"Becky is a witch, but I don't think she's a thief," I said.

"That would be just Becky's style to sneak our good-luck charm out from under us," said Jodi.

"Wait a minute," I said. "Becky's nasty, but she's not sneaky."

"Ti An," said Jodi, "I can't believe you are actually defending Becky. Are you a Pinecone or what?"

I bit my lip. I *hated* having Jodi mad at me, but I love mysteries. I read a lot of mystery books from the library, and it's never the obvious culprit.

**Look for these and other books
in THE GYMNASTS series:**

THE GYMNASTS

#11 MYSTERY AT THE MEET

Elizabeth Levy

AN
APPLE
PAPERBACK

SCHOLASTIC INC.
New York Toronto London Auckland Sydney

ISBN 0-590-42823-3

12 11 10 9 8 7 6 5 4 3 2 1   0 1 2 3 4 5/9

Printed in the U.S.A.   28
First Scholastic printing, May 1990

To the real Thai An, and Hoi.

An Ancient Curse

"Ti An, get your butt in gear," said Patrick as I got ready to practice my vault. I giggled. Patrick is the only person I know who talks to me like that. He talks to me as if I'm not fragile and made out of china so that I'll break. Patrick is my coach at the Evergreen Gymnastics Academy. I'm the youngest girl on my team, the Pinecones, and I'm built real skinny. I just had my ninth birthday. My mom says that I'm going to be tall, at least tall for a Vietnamese, but I sure don't look tall next to the other Pinecones. Patrick says that all pinecones carry the seeds for the evergreens, the tallest trees in the forests of the Rocky Mountains. There are a lot of evergreens in Denver where we live, and I *know* I'm never going to be a big tree.

I'm the youngest, the shortest, and the skinniest Pinecone. My teammates keep telling me that short, young, and skinny are exactly what the judges *love* in gymnasts. The judges certainly never *love* me. It's funny how I can do a trick really well in practice, but at a meet it's as if all my skills fly out the window. Unfortunately we were right in the middle of our competition season. We had had a meet scheduled every other Saturday for nearly two months. So far, we had lost each one. It was a drag.

Patrick keeps telling me that gymnastics would be boring without competition. Personally I don't think boring's so bad. I *hate* the way my stomach feels at a meet. I go into a meet hoping I'm going to do okay, but something *always* happens.

What's so incredible about the Pinecones is that nobody hates me for it. I think I must have the best team in the whole wide world — so what if we don't win many meets.

Darlene Broderick is the oldest and tallest Pinecone. She's incredibly beautiful and talented. Her father is Big Beef Broderick of the Denver Broncos. I don't know much about football, but my father loves it when Big Beef shows up at our meets. Lauren Baca, Cindi Jockett, and Jodi Sutton are all eleven, and make up the rest of the Pinecones. Cindi and Jodi are both tall for their age. They keep telling me that they're jealous of me because I'm so petite. They say I've got the perfect body for gymnastics. Lauren Baca is great. She's built like a powerhouse, but she's short — not as short as me, but she is short.

Ashley Frank is the reason I joined the Pinecones. I live next door to her. We found out that we both loved gymnastics. I didn't love the place where I was taking it. It was in downtown Denver, at Amazons' Gymnastic Center. The gym was a lot more luxurious than Patrick's, but the coach was mean. He kept telling me that I had a lot of talent, then he would yell at me at the top of his lungs when I made a mistake. I told my parents that I wanted to quit gymnastics. My dad had his heart set on my being an athlete. He was sure that I had real talent. But I insisted on quitting. I couldn't imagine gymnastics ever being fun again, but I was so wrong. Just when I had finally talked my dad into letting me quit, Ashley told me about Patrick's gym.

She said the coach was fun. I couldn't imagine a coach who was fun. I thought all coaches were like dragons. Coach Miller at the Atomic Amazons' gym really did remind me of a dragon, breathing fire on me to make me jump. Patrick doesn't breath fire. He never yells at me when I fall apart at a meet. He doesn't even give me a "disappointed" look, and I love him for it. I hope that someday I really put it together for him at a meet.

Today we were working on my handspring vault with a layout. It's supposed to have a long, graceful afterflight — that's how high and how far I travel after rebounding off the horse. I'm supposed to travel at least the length of my body.

All the really interesting vaults have full afterflights, but the longer the afterflight, the harder it is to land on two feet. I hadn't stuck my landing. In fact, I had fallen forward straight on my nose.

"That was great," said Patrick. "Do it like that at the meet, and we'll have the Atomic Amazons quaking."

I couldn't believe that Patrick had actually thought my vault was good.

"It was beautiful," said Patrick.

"I loused up the landing!" I exclaimed.

"But everything else was perfect," he said. "Ti An, I've got a surprise in mind for you and Lauren. I want to start to teach you the Yamashita vault."

"You're kidding!" exclaimed Lauren, sounding all excited. "I thought that only world-class gymnasts could do that!" Lauren gave me a high five.

I slapped her hand, but a little tentatively. Sometimes Lauren can really hurt you when she gets excited.

"I don't think I can do the Yamashita," I said softly to Patrick.

"A couple of years ago I would have said that it was too advanced," said Patrick. "But times have changed in gymnastics. I just read that a well-motivated and well-trained gymnast can indeed master this vault." Patrick's eyes kind of twinkled when he said "well-motivated and well-trained."

"Is that me?" I asked.

"You betcha," said Patrick. "I think you're going to love the Yamashita. It's really just an extension of the handspring. It requires more power and better timing. As your hands hit the vault in the handspring, you whip your legs up in the air in a pike position and just fly."

"It sounds fun," said Lauren.

"It sounds scary," I said.

"Ti An always says that," joked Darlene. "She says it's scary and then she does it."

"She doesn't do it at a meet," muttered Ashley. I guess when I said that none of my teammates razz me about the fact that I do poorly at meets, I should have made an exception for Ashley. It's so queer. Ashley is supposed to be my friend. She's my neighbor, and we're the closest in

5

age — but sometimes she can be more than a little mean.

"Oh, shut up, Ashley," said Jodi.

"I bet you anything that Ti An never does the Yama-foo-foo in a meet," said Ashley.

"Yamashita," I said.

"Well, you grew up pronouncing those names. It's easy for you."

"Yamashita was a Japanese gymnast, not Vietnamese, Ashley," said Patrick. "And if you would stop commenting on everything Ti An does, I'd have a second to try to teach Lauren and Ti An this vault. I'd like to spring it on Coach Miller — maybe not at next week's meet, but at the one after that. Ti An and Lauren should be able to learn this new vault in a month."

Patrick demonstrated the vault. "Okay, Ti An, I'll be spotting you. Try it."

I bit my lip as I started my takeoff for the horse. I hit the springboard as hard as I could. I flew into the air. Patrick pushed my body over the horse, and I kicked my legs above my head in a pike position and then straightened them out to land.

I looked back at Patrick. "Beautiful!" he exclaimed.

My mouth was open. "It's fun!" I exclaimed.

Patrick grinned at me. "That's my girl," he said.

6

"Good going, Ti An," said Jodi when I sat back down with my teammates.

"I still say she'll never do that in a meet," said Ashley.

I glared at her.

"I wish we didn't always have to compete against the Atomic Amazons," said Cindi.

Patrick heard her. "I'm getting tired of that refrain," he said. "The Atomic Amazons can be beaten. You girls have got to stop thinking of them as real-life Amazons. They're all intermediate gymnasts, just like you. I don't set up meets against them just to torture you."

"Are you sure?" asked Lauren. "Maybe you have a hidden desire to punish us for losing so much."

"Lauren, first of all, you girls *have* beaten the Atomic Amazons a couple of times."

"Was Ti An sick then? I don't remember," muttered Ashley.

"No, she wasn't," Lauren argued, sticking up for me. I appreciated what Lauren was doing for me, but it made me feel a little bit ashamed, too.

"Besides, Patrick," argued Cindi, "you haven't explained why we always have to go up against the Atomic Amazons."

Patrick spread his hands wide open. "It's not my fault that they're one of the only other nearby clubs with an intermediate team. It's just a fact of life. I'm sure the Denver Broncos don't complain because they have to play the Los Angeles Raiders every year."

"The Broncos *do* complain," said Darlene.

Patrick shook his head. "Thanks, Darlene." He laughed. "Anyhow, girls, I'm counting on you to set an example. This will be the boys' first meet, and they're bound to be nervous. I want you to show them how to be cool under pressure."

Patrick had recently added a boys' team. Jodi's mom was the coach. Jodi's mom is a super gymnast. She was once on the national team.

"I think the Pinecones should sign a petition — no more Amazons," joked Lauren. At least, I think she was joking. I would love it so much if I never had to face the Amazons again. I was only with the Amazons for six months, but it was the worst six months of my life.

Most of the girls were older than me, but that's true at Patrick's, too. But these girls were so intent on winning that they were scary. After a while, they began to tease me that I was bad luck for the team. It started as a joke, but then I think they started to believe it. One of the girls even went to Coach Miller and told him that she thought I brought bad luck to the team.

Whenever we compete against the Atomic Amazons, I always remember the worst thing Coach Miller ever said. He said, "Ti An isn't bad luck.

She's just one of these kids who leaves her courage on the practice mats." Those words always sounded like an ancient curse to me. Now I was worried that my new teammates might be beginning to think the same thing. Maybe the curse was true.

2

Nerves of Spaghetti

My dad is a professor of history at a community college in Denver. He teaches Asian history, but mostly he teaches about the war in Vietnam. He didn't fight in it. Sometimes stupid kids ask me if my dad ever killed American soldiers. He didn't. He was only twelve years old when he came to the United States with my grandmother. I never knew my grandfather — he died of tuberculosis in prison in South Vietnam, before the North won the war. My grandfather was a very famous man in South Vietnam. He ran for President, before the North won the war. But South Vietnam wasn't anything like America. Here if you run for President and lose, nothing happens to you. But my grandfather knew that it would be very dangerous for him if he lost the election. That's when he sent my father to America. Grandfather lost, and that was when he was put in prison by the man who won. My dad tells me that even when my grandfather was in prison, he exercised every day. When Dad was a boy in Vietnam he ran track at the French school. Dad loves sports. It was Dad who wanted me to start gymnastics.

Mom and Dad were both born in Vietnam. She was only eight years old when she left, but she tells me stories about it all the time. Dad loves the snow in Denver, and he loves to ski, but Mom hates the cold. She misses the warm, humid nights. She says she remembers, as a very little girl, playing outside in the family courtyard every night under the moon. But she also remembers the terrible noise from the bombing, and she hates thunderstorms. I'm scared of thunder, too. Mom never makes me feel like a sissy.

I've never seen Vietnam. Someday I'd like to go. We've got lots of relatives who are still there, cousins I've never met. It's strange to have relatives that you've never seen. Of course, if I met my relatives I'd have to explain to them why I spell my name funny. Most Vietnamese would spell my name "Thai An." When I first learned to spell my name in kindergarten, I started to spell it Ti An because that's the way it sounded. Later,

I liked the fact that it was shorter, and to me it looked more "American." My dad wishes that I would go back to spelling it what he calls the "real" way, but mom says that it's my name, and I can spell it any way that I want. It would be different in Vietnamese letters anyhow. Mom's a little looser than Dad. She doesn't take things quite so seriously. Mom says that because I'm an only child, Dad has a lot "invested" in me and that I have to understand. I don't understand exactly what "invested" means, but I know that Dad is tough on me.

It's hard to do everything exactly the way Dad would want. He's the kind of person who just seems to do everything perfectly. He loves to paint, and he mixes beautiful colors for his paintings, but if a painting isn't perfect, he throws it out. He hates to make mistakes.

Dad runs marathons now, and he's always training to try to run faster. He's very dedicated. Mom likes to run, too, but not so far. Dad comes to every one of my meets. He just got a video camera, and he insists on bringing it to each meet.

"That's what Becky's dad does," I told him. "The Pinecones all think Becky's a jerk." Becky is an advanced gymnast, and she's always picking on the Pinecones.

"Becky Dyson is the best gymnast at your

gym," Dad reminded me. He was right, but it didn't mean that Becky was very nice.

"Just please don't stick the camera in my face when I'm on the beam or doing my vault," I begged Dad.

Mom laughed, a little nervously. "Honey, give your dad a little credit. He can be discreet."

"Thank you," said Dad. "Besides, the camera has a zoom lens. I'll be able to keep my distance. Now, you just be sure that you go the distance."

I rolled my eyes. Sometimes Dad can be so corny. I know that he wants me to do well, and I know that gymnastics lessons are very expensive. I'm grateful and all, because I really do love gymnastics, and I especially love my team. Sometimes I wish that Dad was more like Lauren's dad. He hardly ever comes to meets. Even Darlene's dad, Big Beef, who's a professional athlete, doesn't seem to care as much as my dad does whether we win or lose.

Dad wanted to drive me to the meet. I would really rather have gone with Cindi, who offered to pick me up. Her brother Jared is so nervous about his first meet that he makes me look loosey-goosey. I would have liked to have driven with Cindi, Jared, and her family, but I didn't want to hurt Dad's feelings. We gave Ashley a ride. She had on a brand-new warm-up suit.

"Isn't it cute?" she asked me. It was bright

purple with silver stripes on its sleeves. I thought it was a little loud, but I didn't tell Ashley that.

In fact, I didn't have to say anything to Ashley. Ashley loves to talk. She didn't even wait for me to answer. "I know my new warm-up suit is going to bring me luck," she chattered on.

I just looked out the window. I couldn't wait for the meet to be over. I always feel that way before a meet. The only way I can get through a meet is to tell myself that it will last only three hours. Win or lose, the horrible nervous feeling in my stomach will be gone when the meet is done.

Dad pulled up in front of the Atomic Amazons' gym. It's in a beautiful modern building right next to the Brown Palace Hotel, the fanciest hotel in Denver.

"Ti An, knock 'em dead," said Dad as we pulled up in front of the gym.

Ashley giggled. "It's not a football game, Mr. Truong."

"I know," said Dad seriously. "In gymnastics you compete only against yourself. It's like a track meet. Nobody can beat you but you."

"What about a much faster runner?" I asked. "Even if you run as fast as you can, somebody just might be faster."

Dad frowned at me. "Of course, Ti An, you're right. When I race, I run against professional marathon runners, and I can't beat them. But here you are all at the same level. It's different."

"Your dad's right," said Ashley. "That's exactly what Patrick says. We have to stop thinking of the Atomic Amazons as real Amazons." Ashley is a little bit of a goody-goody. She's always parroting exactly what she thinks grown-ups want to hear.

I opened the car door, wishing that I could just hide in the backseat until the meet was over. Just then, Cindi and her dad pulled up with Lauren and Jared and Jared's friend Ryan.

Jared's face is full of freckles, and he's got Cindi's bright red hair, but underneath the freckles Jared definitely had a slightly greenish look.

"Are you okay?" I asked him.

"He threw up twice on the way over here," said Cindi cheerfully. "We had to pull over on the freeway."

"I'm sorry," I said.

Jared nodded. "I get carsick a lot," he admitted.

"It's nerves," said Cindi. "You're just nervous before your first meet. It's natural."

"If this is natural, I could skip the whole experience," said Jared. "I don't have nerves of steel. I've got nerves of spaghetti."

I giggled. I understood how he felt. I wished I could have made a joke about it. Somehow, seeing Jared look so miserable made me feel a little better. I hoped that didn't make me as mean as Becky or Ashley. I like Jared and didn't *want* him to be sick. It just made me feel better that I wasn't the only person who felt sick before a meet. And I hadn't even thrown up. I liked the idea that Jared and I both had nerves of spaghetti. The problem was that nerves of spaghetti weren't much good against Amazons.

3

Introducing
Terrence Teddy

"Look who I brought for good luck!" said Lauren. We were in the locker room at the Atomic Amazons' club. The walls are all painted pink. Our locker room back at the Evergreen gym just has gray cement-block walls. Most people would say that the Atomic Amazons' gym is ever so much nicer than our gym, but I'll take ours any day. Even coming back just for a visit made me remember all the times that Coach Miller had yelled at me.

Lauren pulled out of her knapsack the rattiest-looking teddy bear I had ever seen. It had hardly any fur left on it, and what fur it did have was matted down. "It's Terrence Teddy time!" exclaimed Lauren.

"I've never seen him before," I said.

"I know," exclaimed Lauren excitedly. "I haven't been bringing him to meets lately, and I realized that was why we were losing. Ti An, you can hold him for luck."

I picked up Terrence in my arms. "He looks awfully skinny," I said.

"He's like you," said Ashley with a giggle. "He's got too little stuffing."

Suddenly I heard a voice behind me bellow, "What is that ratlike animal, Ti An?"

I whirled around. Becky Dyson is thirteen. She is not just tall — she's so muscular that she can look kind of scary. I guess most people would say she's pretty, but I don't think so. I think Cindi with her red hair is much prettier. Jodi's blonde, but there's nothing washed-out-looking about Jodi. Becky never gets tan because she says the sun is bad for you. She says that "real" gymnasts are inside the gym so much that they are supposed to look pale. I don't know where that leaves Darlene and me. Becky never smiles a natural smile. She's either scowling or she's got kind of a sneer on her face. She scares me.

I hugged Terrence to my chest. "This is Terrence," I said. "He's good luck!"

Becky put her hands on her hips. "I don't believe it! The baby of the baby Pinecones brings

18

in a teddy bear to a meet," she sneered. "This is too embarrassing."

I didn't know what to do. If I told Becky that Terrence really belonged to Lauren, then Becky might turn her anger on Lauren, and that wouldn't be nice. Becky really seems to hate Lauren. Me, she usually leaves alone.

"Ti An, you cannot, I repeat, *cannot* bring that rat out onto the gym floor."

"Hold it right there, big mouth," said Lauren, grabbing Becky's elbow. "Terrence brings good luck."

"Terrence Teddy . . . that's the most babyish name I've ever heard."

"I think it was pretty precocious for a two-year-old to call a teddy 'Terrence,' " said Lauren.

"Who cares if Ti An was smart as a baby? She still can't bring that teddy bear out and let the Atomic Amazons see it."

I put Terrence down on a bench.

"Pick him up," Lauren shouted at me. I grabbed him guiltily.

"Put him down," said Becky. I started to put him back on the bench.

Finally Jodi pushed into the circle and grabbed Terrence. "He doesn't belong to Ti An. Stop picking on her," she said. I wished I had stood up to Becky myself.

"Who does that rat belong to?" Becky demanded.

"He belongs to all of us," I said in a shaky voice. Lauren rewarded me with a huge grin.

"He's the Pinecones' good-luck bear," said Jodi, winking at me.

"Well, he's an embarrassment to Patrick and the whole Evergreen team. You can't take him out to the floor."

"I agree with you," said Ashley. "I think Terrence is too, too shabby to bring anybody good luck."

"You're the only Pinecone with good taste," said Becky.

Ashley smirked.

"She's the only Pinecone with the bad taste to like Becky," Jodi whispered to me.

"Becky, stop being so bossy," said Darlene with a yawn. Darlene was tying up her braids with a dark green evergreen ribbon to get them out of her face. "We Pinecones can do anything we want."

"Right," I said, encouraged by Darlene's and Jodi's boldness. "Besides, I read in my gymnastics magazine that Brandy Johnson has a good-luck stuffed animal. If she can have one, why can't we?"

Becky glared at me. "If you're Brandy Johnson, you can do whatever you want. If you're on the

Olympic team at fourteen, you can make a smelly sock your good-luck charm. But if you're a Pinecone — and the littlest Pinecone at that — it just looks babyish and stupid to bring a disgusting teddy bear into the Atomic Amazons' gym."

"I agree with Becky," said Ashley. "We don't want to do anything that would make us look silly."

"You're silly believing any word that Becky says," snapped Lauren.

I had to admit that Terrence was a very shabby-looking stuffed animal. He wasn't bringing us much luck if all we could do was fight over him.

"Maybe we should leave him in the locker room," I suggested as a compromise.

"Never," said Lauren. "Ti An, when are you going to learn that the Pinecones stick together?"

"Hey, Ti An did her part. She told Becky that Terrence belongs to all of us," said Jodi. Jodi won't let *anybody* put down *any* of the Pinecones. She's a great team player.

We trooped out onto the floor. I was still holding Terrence. The judges' table was already set up, and two judges in the official blue blazers from the United States Gymnastics Federation reminded me that there was more at stake here than just a teddy bear.

Patrick was standing in a circle with Jodi's

mother and a little boy who looked about my age. He had dark, curly hair, and he was a little chubby for a gymnast, but he had one of the Atomic Amazons' bright red T-shirts on and white shorts.

"Oh, no," groaned Jodi. "Nick the pest from . . . outer space."

"That doesn't rhyme," I said.

"Who's Nick the pest?" asked Lauren.

"He's Barking Barney's son."

"Barking Barney" owns a chain of pet stores around Denver. I love his radio commercials. They always start out with a riddle about an animal.

I never knew that Barking Barney was a real person until he started to date Jodi's mom. He's the last person in the world that you'd think Jodi's mom would like. He's kind of fat, and he wears gold chains.

"What's Barking Barney's son like?" I asked.

"He's totally obnoxious, and he's decided he wants to be a gymnast, too. He's a copycat. Mom didn't think it would be a good idea for her to coach him, so Barking Barney enrolled him with the Atomic Amazons. All he does is tell me how the Atomic Amazons' beginners boys' team is going to beat the Evergreen team."

Just then, Nick spotted Jodi and the rest of

us. He put his hands on top of his head and waved them, like bunny ears.

"What's he doing?" I asked.

"He's pretending to be a bunny," groaned Jodi.

"Oh, I bet it's because of this week's radio ad," Darlene asked. " 'Why is a rabbit's nose always shiny?' "

" 'Because his powder puff is on the wrong end,' " I answered, giggling.

Jodi gave us a dirty look.

Barking Barney's son hopped over to us — I mean literally hopped. He did a kind of bunny hop over to where we were standing.

"Does he always pretend to be the animal in the ads?" I asked. "I think that's kind of cute."

"He just does that to embarrass me," said Jodi.

"Hi, Jodi-podi," squeaked Nick. I couldn't tell if he was trying to talk like a bunny or if that was his normal voice. "Aren't you going to wish me luck on my first meet? We're going to beat the pants off your boys' team."

"If you're so cocky, you don't need luck," said Jodi with a frown.

"Don't let him touch Terrence Teddy," said Jared, coming over with the boys' team. Quickly I put Terrence behind my back.

"Who's Terrence Teddy?" asked Nick. "Is he somebody really good on your team?"

Jodi giggled. "Exactly, Nick. Terrence Teddy is an incredible gymnast from England, isn't he, Ti An?"

I nodded my head. Sometimes the Pinecones kid me that I take things too literally, but this time I knew that Jodi was just teasing Nick.

"Where is he?" Nick asked. He looked around the gym, nervously.

"He's going to beat the stuffing out of you," said Jodi. "He told us that. He's praticing his secret spell that will turn all the Amazons into jelly."

Nick's lower lip stuck out into a pout. "I'm not scared of anybody named Terrence."

"That just shows how stupid you are," said Jodi. Nick gave her a dirty look.

"I'm not stupid, and my team is going to beat your team."

Suddenly I felt something pull Terrence Teddy out of my arms.

Becky had come behind me and grabbed him. "I told you jerks not to bring *him* out on the floor," said Becky. "Ti An, how dare you disobey me and bring that stupid Terrence out here!"

"We'll do what we want," said Lauren, grabbing Terrence back from Becky. She put him in her knapsack with only his head sticking out.

"I've seen kids in kindergarten with knapsacks like that," muttered Becky.

"A teddy bear," snorted Nick. "So that's who Terrence Teddy is. He's a jerky-looking old teddy bear."

"Terrence stands for excellence," I taunted back.

"Terrence stands for terrible," said Nick. "That's because the Evergreen teams are going to stink something terrible today. I know it in my bones."

I hoped Nick was going to be wrong. But I wasn't sure.

4

No Effort
Too Feeble

My palms were sweaty. I kept trying to take deep breaths, but they sounded more like sighs.

"Relax," said Lauren. "You're going to do fine." I was first up on the very first event of the meet. One reason that I don't worry too much about the fact that I lose at meets is that I'm expected to lose. I'm not just being defeatist. I'm telling the truth. Everybody knows that gymnastics meets are not exactly fair. The first person up doesn't really have the same chance as the last person on a team. All the judges expect the coaches to put their best performers last, so the judges *always* give a lower score to the first one up. Even if I did the most spectacular vault in the whole meet, the judges would probably give me a low score.

Luckily today I wasn't ready to do the Yamashita. I was doing the easier layout handspring vault. Patrick had put me first this time again. If I fouled up, there were five other Pinecones behind me. The judges throw out the lowest score, so even if I completely mess up, I can't hurt the team too much.

Patrick adjusted the vault to make sure it was at the right height and that it was steady. Patrick walked me back along the runway to where I would start the vault. He smiled at me. I couldn't imagine why he would be smiling. I never found anything to smile about at a meet.

"Ti An, look at me," Patrick insisted.

I lifted my face.

"You've done this vault dozens of times in practice. You can do it now."

"Yes, Patrick," I said nodding my head up and down. I could see my father getting in position to videotape my vault. The judges took their positions at the table.

Patrick followed my glance over to my father. "Put everything out of your mind except the mechanics of the vault," he said.

I nodded, not really listening to him. My father waved to me.

"Are you just nodding at me, or are you listening to me?" Patrick asked.

I nodded my head up and down. Patrick shook his head a little at me, as if he realized that I was distracted. He put his arm around me. "Ti An, believe me, you're going to be fine."

I tried to take a deep breath. It came out as a sigh again.

Patrick lifted my chin. "Listen to me. No matter what happens today, it's going to be okay. Just go out there and have fun."

My eyes widened. Patrick was a little bit crazy. Who could imagine having fun when I was just about to be the first one up at a meet?

"Ti An Truong up on the vault. Lauren Baca in the hole. They are both from the Evergreens," said the announcer.

I bit my lip and took my place along the runway. Lauren ran up to me. "Quick," she said. "Touch Terrence on his head for good luck."

Becky was giving us dirty looks. The judges were frowning at me. I was supposed to be getting ready to salute them. My father had the video camera up to his eye.

"I can't right now," I hissed to Lauren. She was embarrassing me by bringing the little teddy bear right up to the vaulting run.

Lauren took a step back. I hadn't meant to hurt

her feelings. I saluted the judge, raising both my hands into the air. I picked up my head, but I didn't look at the judges — that would make me too nervous. I didn't look at Patrick, standing to the side, ready to spot me if I couldn't get over the vault. I tried to empty my mind of everything except my approach.

I ran on my tiptoes, keeping my elbows close to my body so that I wouldn't look like I was flying apart in all directions. I hit the board just right. I flew up in the air. It felt as if I had all the time in the world. I stretched out into a layout, my feet well above my head. I reached out for the horse with my hands. I flipped into a handstand and then pushed down with my hands to begin my afterflight.

That's when my problem began. I didn't have enough propulsion. I felt my legs flipping over too fast, but I couldn't control it. I was scared that I would land flat on my back. That's the one thing that Patrick warns us never to do, because it's so dangerous to fall on your back.

I rolled to my side, knowing that I was completely messing up the vault, but at least I would avoid injury. I landed with most of my weight on my elbow. The pain shot up and down my arm and into my neck.

I got up to my knees and, holding my elbow

with my other hand, I finally stood up. I let go of my elbow to give the judges a weak salute, but my arm hurt like the dickens.

"Are you all right?" Patrick asked. He tried to examine my elbow, but it was hard to let him, it was hurting so much. "You landed right on your funny bone," Patrick said.

"There was nothing funny about it," I said, squinching my eyes together so that they wouldn't tear.

Patrick felt my elbow. "Can you move your arm?" he asked.

I raised it over my head and shook it around. It moved fine, but it still tingled.

"It's okay," I said.

"Do you want to scratch your second vault?" Patrick asked me. "I can tell the judges you hurt yourself." He glanced at the judges who were conferring about my score on the vault I had just messed up.

The judges flashed a 4.4. It wasn't the lowest score I could have gotten, but it wasn't very good. I calculated in my head. If I let this score stand I had really let down the Pinecones. I could move my arm in all directions. It still hurt, but I knew I hadn't injured myself. There's a real difference between pain and injury.

"I can do another vault," I said to Patrick. "I'm sorry I messed this one up. I'll try again."

"Do you want to do an easier vault?" Patrick asked me.

I breathed a huge sigh of relief. I hadn't wanted to suggest it myself, but if Patrick suggested it, it was okay.

"If you don't mind," I said.

"Do a straddle vault," Patrick suggested.

I nodded my head happily. A straddle vault was a lot easier than any vault with a layout. I went back to the start of the runway.

Lauren was still nervously cuddling Terrence. As I passed her I reached out for Terrence and patted him on the head. Lauren smiled at me. "I need some luck," I said.

I ran for the horse again. It should have been easy, but this time I hit the springboard all wrong. I ended up banging into the horse without even going over it. I might as well as not bothered even *trying* a second vault. My first score would be the only one that counted.

I went back to the Pinecones, and sank down cross-legged on the mats. Darlene patted me on the back. "Good try," she said.

"I goofed," I admitted. "Maybe I should have tried the layout vault as my second one. What do you think?"

"Don't worry about it," said Jodi, slapping me on the back. "You did your best."

Lauren put chalk on her hands to make sure

that she wouldn't slip when she hit the horse.

"Good luck," I said to her.

Lauren tapped Terrence on the head, leaving a little white spot right above his forehead. It made him look bald.

We watched Lauren do her vault. She was doing a layout handspring vault, the same one that I had tried. She didn't have as good a pre-flight as I did, and her handspring was wobbly. She had to take two extra steps on her landing.

"Way to go, Lauren!" Jodi shouted, waving her arms in the air as if Lauren had just done the best vault in the world. The Atomic Amazons and Coach Miller gave us dirty looks, as if they couldn't believe we would applaud a teammate for such a feeble effort. That's why I love the Pinecones. No effort is too feeble. It's because we're friends.

5

We Got Sauced

The boys started off as badly as we did. Jared fouled up *incredibly* on his first vault. He turned bright, bright red, and looked so angry that I thought he was going to have a temper tantrum.

So did Cindi. "Uh-oh," she said. "Sometimes when Jared doesn't do well at first, he just gets worse."

"That doesn't sound like Jared," I said.

"Nobody knows him like a sister," said Cindi.

But Jared didn't get worse. Jared did his second vault better than he had ever done it in practice. He seemed to inspire the other boys, because suddenly the boys' team acted as if they couldn't lose. And they couldn't — they were wonderful. We Pinecones started cheering for them at the top of our lungs.

Barking Barney's son, Nick, on the Atomic Amazons' team, was the one who really fell apart. It seemed to me that he was trying tricks that were way too hard for him. But that's Coach Miller's style. He always pushes beginning gymnasts, not to the point where anybody gets hurt, but I knew for a fact that Coach Miller pushed *me* to the point where I was scared all the time.

The more we cheered for the Evergreen boys' team, the better they did. Nick threw us a dirty glance every now and then, but that didn't stop Jodi from yelling her head off for our team. It was good that we had something to cheer about because we Pinecones were slaughtered. The Atomic Amazons wiped the floor with us in each event, but we were so excited for the boys that it hardly seemed to matter. When I was on the Atomic Amazons, if the girls had done poorly and the boys had done well, Coach Miller wouldn't have allowed the girls' team to join in the celebration. At the end of the meet we all ran up to the boys' team to tell them how great they were. Poor Terrence's head was poking out of Lauren's knapsack. He hadn't brought the Pinecones much good luck, but he had sure helped our other teams.

Patrick didn't just have the boys' team to feel

good about. Our advanced team, Becky's team, really creamed the Atomic Amazons. Patrick was incredibly happy, and Coach Miller seemed furious to see his advanced team beaten. It was the third time in a row that Becky's team had beaten the Amazons. Naturally Becky was acting like Queen of the Gymnasts. She couldn't wait to show her trophy to the boys' team. Becky's a little silly about boys. She just loves having a boys' team to show off in front of.

"Let's compare trophies when you get yours," she cooed. She practically pushed the Pinecones out of her way.

"Sorry you guys couldn't make it a sweep for the Evergreens," Ryan said.

"The Pinecones are our own termite brigade," said Becky, giggling. "They always bring the Evergreens down."

"That's enough, Becky," said Patrick.

"Come on, Patrick," said Becky. "Wouldn't it have been great to have had a clean sweep today? If only you had a decent intermediate team, the Atomic Amazons would really be afraid of us . . . especially now that we have such a good boys' team."

"I said that's enough, Becky," warned Patrick.

"You've got to admit she's got a point," I said with a sigh.

Patrick overheard me. "Ti An, Lauren, Cindi —

all the Pinecones, I want to talk to you alone, now."

Patrick herded us into a corner.

"Do you think he's gonna yell at us?" I whispered to Darlene.

"Ten to one, he tells us to turn the page," said Jodi.

I giggled. "It's a bet," I said.

"Pinecones, you've got to put this behind you," said Patrick. "Turn the page."

Jodi winked at me and started to giggle.

"Jodi, losing isn't anything to laugh about," said Patrick.

Jodi turned bright red.

"It was my fault," I said, thinking that I had been the one to giggle first.

"It wasn't *your* fault, Ti An," said Patrick. "You're too quick to take the blame. You got flustered after your first vault."

I realized too late that Patrick had thought I was talking about the meet. I had just felt guilty because I had been whispering with Jodi. It turned out that while Patrick didn't yell at us the way Coach Miller would have, he made me feel twice as bad. I really wanted to win for Patrick.

"The thing that concerns me most," he said, "is that you've lost your confidence. It's wrong for people to say this isn't a good team. You are. I wouldn't trade any of you. But I won't lie to you and say that I'm not worried about our losing streak. We're improving in practice, but we're not improving as a team. We're losing more now than we did in the first half of the meet season. You young gymnasts are better than that."

"We're sorry, Patrick," I said quickly. I was sure he was speaking mainly about me.

"Ti An, I'm not talking just to you. The whole team is experiencing a slump."

"Yeah, I stunk," said Jodi. She had fallen off the beam three times, failed to nail her vault, and had finished her floor routine completely off the music. At least I had done my floor routine without too many mistakes.

"I've never been so sloppy," said Cindi.

"Maybe we're destined never to beat the Atomic Amazons again," I suggested.

"Ti An," interrupted Patrick, "you can't write the Pinecones off by any stretch of the imagination. You've all just got to put aside everything that's bothering you. Now is the time to come together and start doing a topflight job."

"Like the boys did," said Cindi.

Patrick smiled. "Well, I wanted the Pinecones to be an example to the boys, but I guess it worked out the other way around," he said.

We watched as the boys went up to the winner's circle to collect their trophies. Jared was bright red from his workout, but he was laughing. He looked so happy and proud. He waved his medal at Cindi.

My father and mother came out on the floor with the other parents. I noticed that Dad was talking to both Barking Barney and to Cindi's dad. Barking Barney seemed to be in an incredibly happy mood considering that his son had just lost.

"Better luck next time," I said to Nick, feeling a little sorry for him.

"Well, you Pinecones didn't have much luck, either," said Nick in a pipsqueak voice. He gave me a little snort. Maybe I shouldn't have felt sorry for him.

"Besides," continued Nick, "it wasn't fair, 'cause you girls were cheering so loudly."

"Now, Nick, gymnastics isn't war. It's natural that Jodi should cheer for her teammates," said Barking Barney.

I could see that now Jodi was feeling fidgety and nervous. Maybe she was feeling guilty thinking that she should have cheered a little for Nick.

I forgot that Jodi doesn't know the word *guilt*.

"Nick, face it. Your team just got sauced today," said Jodi cheerfully.

"If we got sauced, you got barbecued," retorted Nick.

"Heh, heh, Nick's just got barbecue on the brain," said Barking Barney. "That's because

Jodi's mom and I had a little side bet going on this meet. I said her new boys' team wouldn't beat Nick's team. I lost, so I'm cooking barbecue for everybody on both teams next week."

Jodi grinned. "Well, I have to admit we got the better of that bet. Mom's not a great cook."

"Thanks a lot," said Jodi's mom.

"But you're a great coach," said Jared.

Sarah Sutton grinned. "Thank you, Jared. I think everybody will have a great time at the barbecue. I may not be a good cook, but Barney is."

"I just wish the Pinecones had more to celebrate," said Dad, putting an instant damper on everything. It was as if he felt we needed to be reminded that we had lost. We didn't. I wish Dad could understand that losing isn't the worst thing in the world.

It's a Proven Fact

"Okay, this isn't funny," said Lauren. She was sitting cross-legged in front of the frosted-pink locker, all the contents of her knapsack spilling around her. She looked anything but in a pretty mood.

"What's wrong?" I asked.

Lauren didn't answer me right away. She turned her knapsack inside out. It was obviously empty.

"Where's Becky?" Lauren demanded.

"She's in the Jacuzzi," said Ashley. "Wouldn't it be neat to have a gym with a Jacuzzi?"

"I'm going to 'Jacuzz' her," snapped Lauren.

"Lauren, calm down," said Cindi. "Actually, a Jacuzzi sounds great. Let's all go."

"You guys don't understand!" shrieked Lauren. "Terrence is missing!"

"He didn't bring us much luck anyhow," said Ashley, grabbing a towel. "I'm going to the whirlpool."

"I had him in my knapsack," insisted Lauren. "You all saw me put him in my knapsack right when I started my vault."

"And he was still in it right after the meet," I said. "He was in there when we all went up to congratulate the boys' team."

"Good work, Ti An!" said Lauren excitedly. "Then it must have been right afterward that Becky stole it. I bet she's drowning Terrence right now."

"That would be just Becky's style to sneak our good-luck charm right out from under us," said Jodi.

"Wait a minute," I said hesitantly.

The Pinecones all looked at me. "Uh . . . that doesn't seem like Becky's style," I managed to stammer out. "I mean, Becky's nasty, but she's not sneaky."

"Ti An," said Jodi, a little bit threatening, "I can't believe you are actually defending Becky. Are you a Pinecone or what?"

I bit my lip. I *hated* having Jodi mad at me, but I really didn't think that it was Becky's style. There are a lot of things wrong with Becky. Becky thinks nobody is as good as she is, but to tell the truth she's kind of an up-front person. You might hate her, but you always know what she's thinking. In a weird way, Jodi's a little bit like Becky, except Jodi is like the good witch in *The Wizard of Oz*, and Becky is the bad witch.

"Becky is a witch, but I don't think she's a thief," I said.

"Ti An's got a point," said Darlene, to my great relief. Darlene never thinks nasty thoughts about anybody.

"If it's not Becky, then it has to be Ashley," said Lauren.

"That's right," said Cindi. Cindi had her hands on her hips, as if daring me to disagree with her.

"Ti An can't argue with us about *that*," said Jodi. "Even *you*'ve got to admit that sneaky is *just* Ashley's style."

I bit my lip. I love mysteries. I read a lot of mystery books from the library, and it's never the obvious culprit.

I wasn't sure Ashley would have taken Terrence. Ashley's not much older than I am and, although I know she admires Becky, she's a little bit scared of the other Pinecones. I don't think she would have the nerve to take Lauren's teddy bear. I was worried about my own nerve, however. I didn't think I had the nerve to stand up

42

to Cindi, Jodi, and Lauren and tell them that they were wrong.

"Well," asked Darlene, "Ti An, what do you think?"

"She's just a baby," said Lauren.

"She is not," said Darlene. "Ti An is very smart about people."

My mouth almost fell open. I couldn't believe that Darlene had just said that about me. I loved the idea that it was true, but it just never occurred to me that anybody would think about me like that — that I was very smart about people.

"So," said Darlene, "Ti An, you're the one who's closest to Ashley. What do you think?"

I swallowed hard. "Why would Ashley steal something that was supposed to bring good luck to all the Pinecones?" I asked.

"You'd make a lousy detective," said Cindi. "Ashley wanted all the luck to herself. That's why she stole it."

"I think we should search Ashley's knapsack," said Lauren.

"And Becky's," exclaimed Jodi. "It's got to be in one or the other."

Lauren headed right over to Ashley's knapsack. "You look in Becky's," she commanded Cindi.

"I don't think you should do that," I said. My

43

voice came out shaky and wimpy.

"Now what, Ti An? Are you scared that Ashley and Becky are going to come back from their Jacuzzi and catch us?" demanded Cindi. "Who cares?"

"You wouldn't want Becky to go through your knapsack if she thought you had something of hers," I said to Lauren.

Lauren stopped her hand on the zipper of Ashley's knapsack.

"Ti An's right," said Darlene. "Besides, I don't even think it's constitutional."

"Are you and Ti An suddenly lawyers, for goodness' sake?" complained Lauren, but she put down the knapsack. "It's a proven fact that lawyers just coddle criminals. Do you want Becky and Ashley to get away with it?"

I shook my head. "I just think you should have more than a suspicion before you go through their stuff." I bit my lip nervously. It was hard standing up to Lauren. She was the one I liked the most of the Pinecones. "I don't think it's right to go through their knapsacks when they're not here," I said. My voice still came out all breathy and almost whispery. I wasn't trying to be a goody-goody, but it just seemed wrong to me.

"I guess Ti An's got a point." Lauren gave me a half-lopsided grin. "Ti An, why do you have to be so dog-garned fair?"

"What's a dog in a garden got to do with it?"
I asked. "Dogs in gardens aren't usually fair.
They like to dig up gardens."

Darlene started to giggle. "Ti An, you are so
cute sometimes."

Even Lauren started to giggle. "Dog-garned,"
she repeated. "It's not a dog in a garden. It's just
something people say when they're trying not to
swear."

"I'm sorry I made you so mad that you wanted
to swear," I told Lauren.

Lauren grinned at me, making me feel better.
"I wasn't mad at you. Well, maybe a little, but
you were right. I shouldn't have taken the sneaky
approach; that's just like Becky and Ashley, the
two sneak thieves who took Terrence. We've got
to go right into the Jacuzzi and confront the
teddy bear thieves directly."

"Oh, boy," said Jodi. "Let's go . . . I can't wait
until Becky confesses."

"She might not have done it," I said hesitantly.

"Well, we'll have a good time asking her," said
Jodi, rubbing her hands together.

7

Showdown
in the Jacuzzi

The jets from the Jacuzzi were so loud that no one heard us come in. Becky's arms were stretched out along the sides of the tub, and her head was lying back. She looked perfectly relaxed. Becky was sitting next to one of the Atomic Amazons who had beaten us. Their trophies lined the edge of the pool. I guess they hadn't wanted to let them out of their sight. Ashley bobbed up and down, letting the bubbles break over her head.

"Uh-oh," said Becky, opening her eyes. "I don't think this Jacuzzi is big enough for all of us."

"Sure it is," said Jodi, dipping her feet in. "Ouch, this _is_ hot."

"It's the perfect temperature," said Becky.

"Everything about this afternoon was perfect."

"Including the perfect crime?" asked Lauren, slipping right into the bubbles.

I followed Lauren into the Jacuzzi. While Becky could sit on the ledge with her head above water, I was too short. I was into bubbles over my head.

I popped up shaking the hot water from my pigtails. Becky laughed at me. "What's the matter, Ti An? Did you get in over your head, the way you did in the meet?"

"Forget bullying Ti An for a minute," said Jodi. "We want to know what you did with Terrence?"

Becky closed her eyes and stretched her legs out into the Jacuzzi, kicking me by mistake — at least, I thought it was a mistake.

"I couldn't be less interested in that ratty-looking teddy bear," said Becky. "I told you not to bring him to the meet, and he *certainly* didn't help you. In fact, I think you should call him your bad-luck teddy."

"He was in my knapsack, and now he's missing, and I'm positive you took him," accused Lauren.

Becky winked at the Atomic Amazon girl. "The Pinecones will look for any excuse to explain why they lost," she said. "You'll have to excuse them."

"Becky, no excuses," warned Lauren. "Tell me what you did with him."

Becky kicked her feet up into the bubbles.

"You're the one who's looking for excuses. Don't you girls know it's bad taste to make excuses for why you didn't win, especially in front of the other team?"

"Sorry," I said quickly to the other Atomic Amazon. I recognized her from when I used to take classes. Her name was Jessica, and she wasn't a very good gymnast. She had been on my team, but she had never seemed to like me very much. She was in high school, pretty old to be in the beginning group still, but Coach Miller makes people stay in a lower group longer than most coaches do. He *says* that he does it to make better gymnasts, but I think he does it so that he can win more meets.

"With Ti An on their team, they don't need any excuses," said Jessica.

"Well, I've had enough," said Becky. "It's not good to stay too long in a Jacuzzi. I'd hate to see the Pinecones turn into the California Raisins." Becky snorted. She pushed out of the pool making a big splash, forcing the water over the sides of the tub.

"Good going, Becky," said Jodi. "You almost drowned your trophy."

"You haven't admitted taking Terrence!" protested Lauren.

"And I'm not going to, because I didn't, stupid. I like collecting trophies, not teddy bears."

48

Jessica snickered. "I'd better get going, too," she said, grabbing her trophy. "We *never* got to win one of these when Ti An was on our team."

"Hey, you!" shouted Darlene. Jessica turned around. "Your hands are turning green. Your trophy turns green if water hits it."

Both Jessica and Becky looked alarmed. Jessica moved the trophy from hand to hand as if it were a hot potato. "What are you talking about? My hands aren't green."

"Oh, whoops," said Darlene. "I guess it must have been you who was turning green with jealousy."

"Why would I be jealous of *you*?" exclaimed Jessica.

"Because the next time our two teams meet, you're going to be sauced," said Darlene.

Jessica just laughed, and followed Becky out of the room.

"I don't think you scared her," said Ashley. "Why did you brag like that? The next time we meet the Atomic Amazons, they'll probably beat us again."

"I couldn't let her beat up on Ti An," said Darlene. "Ti An, how did you ever survive being on a team with that creep?"

The hot, chlorinated water made my eyes sting and turn red, at least I hoped that was what Darlene would think, because her kind words made me want to cry. What would happen to me if my beloved Pinecones ever started thinking I was bad luck?

"I didn't think she was so creepy," said Ashley. "She was the girl who won the all-around trophy in our class."

"Winners can be creeps, too, Ashley," said Darlene. "When are you going to learn that?"

"Speaking of creeps, Ashley," said Lauren. "I want you to give back Terrence."

"Honestly, Lauren, you are such an infant sometimes," said Ashley, sounding a lot like Becky. "I didn't take your stupid teddy bear."

"You did, too," said Lauren.

"Did not!" said Ashley.

"Did too," spit out Lauren.

They sounded like two-year-olds.

"I know it was you," said Lauren.

"Lauren, I didn't touch your stupid teddy bear," said Ashley. She flounced out of the Jacuzzi.

The rest of us sat in the hot tub, staring at each other. "Well," said Jodi, "we didn't exactly get Terrence back."

"At least we warned them that we're on to them," said Lauren. She started walking very slowly up and down the length of the Jacuzzi, pushing her hands through the bubbles. She bumped into Cindi.

"What are you doing?" Cindi asked her.

"I think they've hidden Terrence on the bottom," said Lauren. "Maybe they tied a weight to poor Terrence's paw and drowned him."

"Lauren," said Darlene, "I think your imagination is getting away from you."

"Yeah, well, why don't you help me search?" said Lauren. "I know Ashley or Becky took him, and they were both in the Jacuzzi. I just can't see him because of the bubbles."

"There's an easy way to find out if he's here," I said. I jumped out of the water, went to the wall switch, and turned off the Jacuzzi.

Slowly the bubbles subsided. "Good thinking, Ti An!" exclaimed Jodi as if I had just done something brilliant.

The water soon became still so that you could see the jets along the side and the drain at the bottom.

There was no drowned teddy bear.

"So you see, Lauren, Terrence isn't here," I said. "It wasn't Becky or Ashley."

"This doesn't prove a thing," said Lauren. "It just means that the two of them are smarter than we thought. They've got him hidden somewhere."

"Maybe they're going to send you a ransom note," said Jodi. I looked at her to see if she was joking, but she seemed to be serious.

"Perhaps Terrence is just lost," I argued. "The Atomic Amazons have a huge gym. Maybe Terrence is still outside."

"I looked everywhere," pouted Lauren.

"But with all of us looking, it'll be easier," I said.

We quickly went back into the locker room. I searched the locker room area. Terrence wasn't there. We searched the entire gym from top to bottom, but there was no sign of Terrence.

I looked under all the apparatuses. I searched under the pile of mats. All of the Pinecones helped me.

"Ti An," said a voice that I would always be afraid of. I looked up. Coach Miller was standing over me. "What are you doing?"

"My teammate lost her teddy bear," I stammered. "Have you seen him?"

"No, of course not," said Coach Miller impatiently. "And I don't like Patrick's girls sneaking around my gym after a meet."

"We're not sneaking," I said to Coach Miller in a shaky voice. Lauren and the other Pinecones were standing behind me as if they were much more scared than I was.

"Come on, Ti An," urged Lauren, pulling on my arm. "Terrence isn't here. Let's go. Besides, we know Terrence isn't here because we know who took him." Lauren glared at me. "Becky or

Ashley probably took him home in their knapsacks, *which* we didn't look inside."

The only reason Lauren suspected them was because she didn't like them. Becky and Ashley aren't lovable, but proof is important. Without proof, all we had was suspicion, and I knew how it felt to be the one that everybody suspected. It had happened to me when I had first joined the Pinecones. Someone was spying for the Amazons, and since I had just come over from the Amazons, I was the natural suspect. Luckily Lauren had finally set up a trap and caught the real culprit.

But I'm not Lauren. I'm much shier than she is. I didn't have the guts to argue anymore. I was too worried that they'd stop suspecting Ashley and Becky and start suspecting me.

8

Teddy Bears on the Brain

"Ti An and Lauren, I want you to practice the Yamashita for the next meet in two weeks," said Patrick, looking down at his clipboard.

"Why don't we just forfeit now and get it over with?" muttered Ashley.

"I hate to agree with the twerp, but she's got a point," said Jodi.

Patrick put down his clipboard. "Girls, that kind of defeatist attitude won't get you anywhere. We didn't do well at the meet last weekend, but *I* know that you're a lot better than that. Ti An, get up here. Let me see the Yamashita."

Patrick has always said that there are some tricks in gymnastics that are easier for some of us. The Yamashita is a spectacular vault. If I watched someone else do it, I would think that it was way out of my league. But when I tried it myself, it was as if it fit me like a glove. Maybe it's because I don't weigh very much and I have short legs compared with the rest of my body. The vault just wasn't that hard for me.

I ran for the horse and hit the springboard with a huge bounce. I did the vault okay, but I fell back on my rear end on the landing. I turned and looked at Patrick. "Sorry."

Patrick took three long steps and helped me up where I had landed on the mats. "Ti An, your afterflight was spectacular. You flew as far after your vault as you did getting to the horse. That's what the judges love."

"They aren't going to love me landing on my rear end," I said.

Patrick shook his head impatiently. "That's not the point. You almost did the landing right. The only way you were able to put the brakes on the speed you generated was to lean back on your landing. Now you've just got to fight the tendency to fall back, and you'll stick the landing. The judges are going to be wowed by this vault."

I went to sit down and watch Lauren try the vault. "Good going," Darlene said to me.

"Thanks." I knew the vault had been good. I waited for somebody to say, "Yeah, but Ti An won't do it that way in the meet," but nobody did.

Lauren couldn't get the timing for the Yamashita right. She tried to pike too soon, and she might have really hurt herself if Patrick hadn't caught her.

"I'll never get this," muttered Lauren as she sat back down.

"Sure you will," I assured her.

"It looks so easy when *you* do it," said Lauren.

Patrick called me up to practice the vault again. This time when I landed, I made a windmill motion with my arms, and I was able to keep my balance.

"That's the idea," said Patrick.

"I look like a helicopter," I said.

"A little," Patrick admitted, "but you got the landing. I think we're going to shock the judges and Coach Miller when I have you do that vault in the next meet."

"I'm not going to have to do the Yamashita that soon, am I?" I asked worriedly.

"That's my plan," said Patrick.

"I've got a better plan," said Cindi. "The plan is that we never have to go against the Atomic Amazons again."

Patrick frowned. "No, Cindi, that's not the

plan, and that doesn't even sound like you."

"Sorry, Patrick," said Cindi, "but it's just not fun going to meets and losing."

"It's because Terrence is gone," said Lauren. "Whoever stole him took the stuffing out of the Pinecones." Lauren glared at Ashley.

"Why are you looking at me?" Ashley protested.

"Because Becky isn't in our group," said Lauren. Lauren glared across the floor where Becky was practicing her beam routine. "If you call Becky over here, I'd accuse her to her face."

"Lauren!" exploded Patrick. I had never seen him so angry. "I have had it up to here with you girls sniping at each other."

To my surprise, Lauren wasn't scared by Patrick's angry tone. "Then tell Ashley to give back Terrence. She took him as a joke."

Patrick put his clipboard down. "Will somebody please explain to me what is going on?" he insisted.

"Terrence, my good-luck teddy, got taken at the Atomic Amazon meet," said Lauren. "And we know who took him!"

"How?" insisted Patrick in a low voice.

"How?" repeated Lauren. "Do you mean how did they take it? I don't know. Terrence was in my knapsack, and then he disappeared."

"I meant *how* do you know who took him," insisted Patrick.

"I didn't take him," insisted Ashley. "I didn't go near him."

Lauren just glared at her.

"Becky was making fun of us before the meet," said Jodi. "She said Terrence was too embarrassing to bring out in front of the Atomic Amazons and Ashley agreed with her."

"All of you, listen to me," said Patrick. "I will *not* tolerate my teams endlessly accusing one another."

"I *know* Becky took him," protested Lauren. "If she didn't, then she got Ashley to do her dirty work for her."

"Lauren, this has gone far enough," warned Patrick. "I want you to settle this once and for all."

"Fine," said Lauren. "Call Becky over and see if she has the nerve to deny in front of you that she took Terrence."

"Will that end it?" Patrick asked.

Lauren nodded.

Patrick walked over to the beam where the advanced group was working.

"Patrick sounded really angry," I warned Lauren.

"Well, so am I," said Lauren. "Patrick should know the truth."

"But *you* don't know the truth," I whispered to Lauren.

"Ha!" said Lauren.

Patrick came back with Becky. He was still scowling. "I want to get to the bottom of this and to have no more accusations swirling around *my* gym." The way Patrick said "my" gym made us realize he wasn't fooling around. Most of the time Patrick talked about it as "our" gym.

"Okay," said Becky, shifting her weight from one foot to the other, "what *is* this about?"

"You know," growled Lauren. "It's Terrence. It's time to 'fess up. You took him at the meet, and you've got to give him back."

"Yeah, you wouldn't dare lie in front of Patrick," warned Jodi. I wanted to tell Jodi to just keep quiet and wait and see what Becky said.

Becky didn't even glance at Lauren or Jodi. She looked Patrick straight in the eye. "I never took their silly teddy bear. I didn't touch him. I don't know anything about him. That's it . . . that's all I can tell you."

"But . . . but," sputtered Lauren.

I put a warning hand on her elbow. I knew Patrick would get really mad at her if she said anything now.

"Thank you, Becky," said Patrick. "I believe you."

"May I get back to my beam routine?" asked Becky, sweetly. "I want to make sure I've got my new routine down. I want to win again. I want to win another trophy for the Evergreens."

She sounded sweet, but I knew she was just rubbing it in how few trophies the Pinecones had been able to contribute to Patrick's trophy case.

Patrick isn't dumb. He knew what Becky was saying. "Go back to the beam, Becky," he said. "The Pinecones don't need any more inspirational speeches. I'll do the inspiring. All of you, I want this to be the last I hear about any accusations. Lauren, I'm sorry that Terrence is missing. I can understand that you're upset, but you're going to have to accept your loss."

"Tell her to learn from Ti An," said Becky. "She's good at accepting losses."

My head jerked forward. I couldn't believe Becky could be so nasty. I looked around at my teammates, but nobody said anything to defend me this time. I wanted to cry, but I wouldn't give Becky the satisfaction.

"Becky," said Patrick, angrily, "that was totally uncalled for. Please apologize to Ti An."

"Sorry," mumbled Becky.

"Sorry doesn't do me much good," I said.

Patrick shook his head. "Ti An, Becky, all of you. I will not tolerate any more sniping, cattiness, and accusations." Patrick stretched his arm way over his head. "Girls, I cannot run a gym with this kind of behavior. It has to stop. Do you hear me?"

"Yes, Patrick," we Pinecones all said in unison.

"Becky, I want no more nasty comments from you. Girls, I want no more false accusations. We have a lot of talent in this room that is going to waste. You're spending all your energy fighting each other. Let's save some of that fighting spirit to use against the Atomic Amazons."

"Well, the Pinecones need something," said Becky, flouncing her blonde curls as she passed us. "You Pinecones have teddy bears on the brain."

"I guess that shows how much Becky listened to Patrick," I whispered.

"How could Becky lie with such a straight face!" whispered Lauren.

I couldn't believe Lauren. How could she accuse Becky again right after Patrick's lecture? Hadn't she heard a word of what he was saying? And how could Lauren be so sure that Becky was lying? Becky was right. We did have teddy bears on the brain, and it was tearing Patrick — and us — apart.

9

Vaulting Lawyers

"I can't believe that Becky would have the nerve to just lie like that in front of Patrick," said Lauren.

"Lauren, drop it, already," I said. Lauren had been repeating the same line for the past week. Unfortunately Terrence had still not reappeared. We had called the Atomic Amazons' gym every day to ask if anyone had found him. Finally someone at Coach Miller's office had actually told Lauren, "Don't call us. We'll call you if we find your bear."

My dad was driving us over to Jodi's house, where Barking Barney was going to pay off his debt to Jodi's mom by cooking barbecue for all the Evergreens and the Atomic Amazons. The party was supposed to start at two o'clock, and we were a little early. My dad hates to be late for anything. I was glad that Lauren had asked me for a ride. I didn't want to go to the barbecue by myself. I knew that I'd be practically the youngest person there, and I get shy at big parties. I haven't been to too many, and sometimes it seems like everybody knows how to laugh and joke around except me. I like to make jokes with my friends, the kids I know real well, but it's hard when it's a big group.

"You don't understand," moped Lauren. "Terrence and I have been together since the day I was born."

"I think it is terrible that your Terrence is gone," said Dad, surprising me by being so sympathetic to Lauren.

I glanced over at Lauren. She had her arms crossed and she was scowling like she was still in a bad mood. The loss of Terrence really had depressed her. It was as if Lauren thought that all her good luck had flown out the window. Lauren isn't happy all the time, not the way that Jodi seems, but usually Lauren is quick to giggle. It was hard to imagine her giggling now.

"Cheer up!" I said. "Barbecue beef and ribs will be good for you." I knew that Lauren loved food almost more than anything.

"Those were Terrence's favorite foods," said Lauren sadly.

"You fed your teddy bear barbecue?" I asked incredulously.

"He did get very sticky," admitted Lauren. "I had to put him in the washing machine. That's when he started to lose his fur."

"I think it is very sad to lose your favorite animal," said Dad. "I can understand why you would be so upset."

"Thanks, Mr. Truong," said Lauren.

"When I was a little boy I had a stuffed elephant," said Dad.

"I thought maybe you would have had a real elephant in Vietnam," said Lauren.

Dad smiled. "No, there aren't too many elephants left in Vietnam. This elephant was named Babar. I used to love all the Babar books. My father bought him for me on a trip to France."

"Mom and Dad have been reading me books about Babar the Elephant since I was a baby," I said. "Now, I'm the one who has a stuffed elephant. He's bright green. Except I kept hearing all the TV ads for Barbie so I named him Barbie."

"It's not a very good name for the King of the Elephants," said Dad. "Barbie."

"Well, at least you still *have* Barbie," said Lauren bitterly. "The worst thing is that we know who took Terrence but we can't prove it."

I lay my head back on the car seat and let out a little groan of exasperation. Dad glanced over at me. "What's wrong, Ti An?" he asked.

Lauren didn't give me a chance to answer. "Ti An thinks I'm not being fair," said Lauren. "If somebody stole your Babar wouldn't you want revenge?" Lauren asked.

"Of course," said Dad.

"Dad," I pleaded, "you don't understand. We *don't* know who took it."

"Speak for yourself," said Lauren. "There're only two choices, and if it was Ashley, you know that Becky put her up to it."

"Speaking of Ashley," said Dad, "shouldn't we have been giving her a ride, too?"

"She didn't want one. She's getting a ride with Becky," I muttered. I knew the very mention of Becky would set Lauren off again.

"Naturally they would want to go together," said Lauren, as if that in itself were the proof she was looking for.

"Ti An," said Dad, "have you helped Lauren search for the person who took her Terrence?" The way that Dad asked made me squirm. You have to know my father to understand what he means behind his words. He wasn't just asking "Have you helped Lauren look for Terrence?" He was really asking me, "Ti An, why haven't you found Terrence for Lauren?"

"Sure, she has," said Lauren, making me feel a little better. "Ti An searched the Jacuzzi. We searched the Atomic Amazons' gym. But we didn't search Ashley's or Becky's knapsacks. Ti An didn't want me to do that."

"Why not?" asked Dad.

"Dad! Haven't you heard of the U.S. Constitution?" I asked.

Dad laughed. "I think, Ti An, you'll make a very good lawyer," he said.

I don't know why it felt as if Dad were insulting me. It was as if he thought I didn't care enough about Lauren and Terrence. All I knew was that I wanted to change the subject. Luckily, as obsessed as Lauren had been lately about Terrence, she must have sensed that talking about Terrence's disappearance in front of Dad was making me feel creepy.

She grinned at me. "I want to be a lawyer when I grow up," she said. "We can start a firm, Baca and Troung."

"We can be known as The Vaulting Lawyers," I said.

"Right," said Lauren. "We can advertise, 'We don't put you behind bars — we teach you to fly on bars. . . .' "

"You two girls are being very silly," said Dad.

Lauren giggled. I did, too. Sometimes silly is so much better than serious. The problem is I don't think my dad would ever understand that silly is fun.

10

"Found a Peanut . . . in a Pinecone"

Jodi lives in one of the town houses near the Evergreen Mall. Jodi's whole family are gymnasts. Her mom and dad used to own their own gymastics club in St. Louis. Jodi's sister is a gymnast and a cadet at the U.S. Air Force Academy in Colorado Springs. Jodi loves her sister, but she hates the fact that everybody thinks that Jennifer is just about perfect. Jodi is far from perfect. When I first met her and heard she came from such an incredible gymnastics background, I thought Jodi was going to be Olympic material. But Jodi isn't that good. Somehow I find that a little bit reassuring.

Jodi and her mom moved to Denver after her mom and dad got divorced. Jodi hasn't talked about it too much, but I don't think she's too happy about her mom dating Barking Barney. Personally I think it's neat to know somebody who owns a pet store.

Jodi was sitting out on her front steps when we drove up. There was nobody else around.

She jumped off the porch. "I'm so glad you guys are here," she said to Lauren and me.

"Are we the first?" I asked, a little embarrassed.

"Yeah, except Nick the pest has been here all morning, and he's been driving me nuts."

"Well, at least Becky wasn't the first," said Lauren. "I don't know why Barking Barney *had* to invite her."

"He insisted the bet was for everyone," complained Jodi. "I don't know where we're going to put everyone, but he told Mom to invite all the gymnasts at the Evergreen Gymnastics Academy, and he had Nick invite the entire Atomic Amazons' club. Luckily a bunch of kids couldn't come. Altogether there are about thirty kids coming to this barbecue."

"Is your mom mad about having all these people?" I asked.

Jodi shrugged. "Naw . . . Barney's doing all the work. He even brought some help from his stores to clean up."

"Two-legged or four-legged help?" I asked.

Jodi giggled. "Two-legged. They're college kids who work in Barking Barney's stores."

"There's something I've got to ask you," Lauren said nervously. I looked at her. I wondered if she was going to bring up Terrence again. "What should we call Barking Barney to his face?"

"I'm going to call him Mr. Josephson," I said.

"He'll tell you to call him Barking Barney," said Jodi. "He *likes* people to call him that. That's what I call him."

"Does your mom call him Barking Barney?" Lauren asked.

Jodi shook her head. "No, she refuses. She calls him Barney.

"He's not so bad," admitted Jodi. "He's actually kind of nice to me. If only he didn't come in a package deal with the pest. Talk about names. Nick thinks he's so creative because he made up the rhyme Jodi-podi. I hate that name."

"I don't blame you," said Lauren. "It's bad enough to have to see the Atomic Amazons at the meets. It must be awful to have one hanging around your house."

"Well, it's better than having Nick at the Evergreen club, believe me. If Mom had told Nick that he could work out at Patrick's I think I would have died," said Jodi.

"Oh, Jodi-podi," yelled a high, squeaky voice from the back of the house. I could smell the barbecue from the grill.

"Quick!" said Jodi. "Let's go up to my room — maybe he won't follow us in there."

"Do you have to sneak around your own house?" I asked.

"You don't know what it's like," complained Jodi. "Every two minutes he wants something. And he can't wait a minute. He seems to think that waiting a minute is going to kill him. *I'm* going to kill him."

Lauren and I looked at each other and started to giggle. "What are you two laughing at?" Jodi asked impatiently.

"It's just that Nick sounds a little like you," said Lauren. "You *hate* to wait for anything."

Jodi looked indignant for a moment, and then she too began to giggle.

"Come on," she said. "Let's go to my room." We took the stairs two at a time and went right up to Jodi's room. It's a great room. She's got a practice beam that her sister used to use. I looked at her bookshelves, which were full of trophies that her mom and her sister won. We were only in Jodi's room for about two minutes when there was a knock on the door.

Jodi opened it, and Nick tried to come charging in. Jodi tripped him. "Hold it right there," she insisted.

"There you are, Jodi-podi," said Nick, ignoring Jodi's obvious hostile tone. "Dad told me to go find you and play with you while they finish the barbecue."

"Look, Pesticide," said Jodi. "My name is not Jodi-podi."

"Yeah," said Lauren. "You'd better not call her that, or you'll have all the Pinecones to deal with, not just Jodi."

I shifted my feet uneasily. Lauren is an only child. I am, too, but I knew enough to realize little kids just love attention, and they don't care how they get it. Nick didn't care how mad Jodi got at him. He just wanted her to realize he was there. The best plan would be just to ignore him, but I didn't think I could get Jodi and Lauren to do that.

"The Pinecones are peanuts," said Nick as if he had just said the wittiest thing in the world. "Found a pea-nut . . . found a pea-nut . . . they were Pinecones . . . found a peanut in a Pinecone. . . ."

"Just shut up," yelled Jodi.

"Hee, hee," giggled Nick.

I was beginning to agree that Nick the pest was a good name for him.

"I *am* going to strangle you," threatened Jodi.

Suddenly Nick stopped giggling. "You can't," he said seriously. "Your mom would yell at you."

"Yeah, but you wouldn't be around to hear her," snapped Jodi.

"Besides," said Nick, "your mom said that I was supposed to come and play with you until the other guests came."

"She and your dad probably were trying not to roast you in the fire," said Jodi with a sigh. "Well, you can't come in here."

"Sure I can," said Nick.

"No, you can't," said Jodi. "I told you before . . . my room is off-limits to pests. It's been sprayed with pesticides. No pests allowed."

Nick stuck out his lower lip. "I'll tell your mom that you didn't want to play with me," he threatened.

Jodi slammed her fist down on her desk. Luckily just then the doorbell rang.

"You're saved by the bell," Jodi muttered as she went to the door.

Suddenly the whole party arrived at once. Darlene and Cindi and Ryan and Jared were at the door, along with a whole group of gymnasts from the Atomic Amazons' club.

Soon the entire house filled up. We went out to the backyard to talk to everybody. I don't know who it was who decided that we had to have a game of leapfrog, but nobody in the world is better at doing leapfrog than a bunch of gymnasts. We kept leaping higher and higher, and then it became a contest to see who could do the silliest leaps.

Some of the Atomic Amazons really got into it. They were giggling and laughing. It really didn't matter which team you were on originally. We all kept trying to top each other with silly leaps.

Barking Barney announced that his barbecue ribs were ready. They were incredibly delicious. We sat down in a big circle. It turned out that as gymnasts we all had a lot more in common than we thought. We talked about being nervous before meets and about how hard it was to eat on the day of the meet. Mostly we talked about food. Apparently all gymnasts like to eat.

The Atomic Amazon girls were all impressed when they found out that Jodi's mom was once a nationally ranked gymnast.

"Where are her trophies?" asked one of them. "I didn't see them when we came through the living room."

"Mom doesn't like to show them off," explained Jodi. "In fact, when she first moved here, she didn't take them out of storage. Finally I got her to let me take out one box of them. They're up in my room."

"Neat," said Jessica. Then she snickered to

Becky, "I guess Jodi's got plenty of room up there because she's got no trophies of her own." It was one of those loud whispers that everybody could hear.

"Hey, can we see those trophies?" asked another of the Atomic Amazons.

Jodi looked a little annoyed. I couldn't blame her. The nasty crack about not having any trophies of her own must have hurt. There was no graceful way now for Jodi to get out of showing everybody her mom's trophies. "Sure," she said. "We can go after dessert, if you still want."

"No, let's go now," said Jessica. "We need the exercise before we eat any more."

"Climbing up one flight of stairs isn't much exercise," muttered Jodi, but all the girls got up to go to Jodi's room. Jared noticed we were leaving. Jared tends to notice whenever Darlene is going anywhere. Everybody knows that he has a crush on Darlene.

"Where are you going?" he asked.

"We're going up to see Jodi's mom's trophies," said Jessica.

"Hey, we want to see those," said Jared. "Maybe they'll inspire us."

"You don't need any more inspiration," said Jessica. "You boys already beat our team." She giggled even though she hadn't said anything funny.

74

"It's just a tiny room," explained Jodi, sounding exasperated. "I'm not taking tours up to my bedroom."

"We just want a peek," said Jared. "After all, your mom's *our* coach."

"Okay, come on," said Jodi. "I guess you can all take a look. But I mean it. Everybody won't fit in at once."

"Go on, kids," said Jodi's mom. "It doesn't take long to look at trophies. They all look alike. When you come back down, we'll have dessert ready."

We all started to climb the stairs. I was right behind Jodi when she flung open the door to the room.

Jessica and another of the Atomic Amazons pushed their way past me into the room.

"What's that teddy bear doing up with the trophies?" asked Jessica.

And that's when Lauren pushed past everybody. She lunged for the bookshelf, screaming *"TERRENCE!"*

11

At Least
It's a Plan

"Out! Everybody out!" screamed Jodi. I'm lucky I'm small. I managed to wedge myself around Jessica and looked into Jodi's room.

"Get everybody out of here," hissed Jodi to me as she half pushed Jessica out the door.

"I don't get it," said Jessica.

"Uh . . . sorry, everybody," I said quickly. I shut the door. Lauren was cuddling Terrence in her arms and looking at Jodi in shock.

"Don't look at me like that!" demanded Jodi. "I didn't put him there!"

"What was he doing on your bookshelf?" Lauren demanded.

"Lauren, you can't possibly think that I took Terrence," shouted Jodi. "That would be crazy!"

There was a knock on the door. "Whoever it is, make them go away," growled Jodi.

I went to the door. It was Darlene and Cindi. "What's going on?" Darlene asked.

"Uh . . . it's hard to explain," I whispered.

"Is Jodi okay?" Cindi demanded.

I looked back at Jodi, who had sunk down and was sitting on the beam with her head in her hands. Lauren was on the bed, still cuddling Terrence and not looking at Jodi.

"She's sort of okay," I said to Cindi.

"What does 'sort of okay,' mean?" demanded Cindi.

"Who is it?" Jodi asked.

"It's Cindi and Darlene," I answered.

"Tell them Lauren thinks I'm a thief," said Jodi.

"I do not," said Lauren from the bed.

"Ti An!" insisted Darlene. "What's going on in there?"

"I told you . . . it's very confusing." I turned back to Jodi. "Can't they come in? They're Pinecones after all . . . they're worried about you."

Jodi raised her head. "If you let them in, they'll just suspect me the way Lauren does."

"Cindi and Darlene are your friends," I said to Jodi. "You've got to let them in. We're all Pinecones together." The truth was I was a little scared to be in the room alone with just Jodi and

Lauren squared off against each other. I'm just a little kid. Cindi and Darlene would know how to handle the situation.

"If you had just told me you wanted to borrow Terrence, I would have let you," said Lauren.

"I didn't take Terrence," said Jodi, half yelling again.

Darlene knocked on the door. "Ti An, what's going on?" she insisted.

Jodi sighed. "You might as well let them in, Ti An," she said. "Soon the whole stupid party will know what's going on."

I opened the door with a sigh of relief. Jared, Ryan, and the rest of the boys were still trying to get through. "Go away," I said to the boys. "Jodi will bring down her mom's trophies later."

"What's the big mystery?" asked Jared.

"There's no mystery," I said, but I was lying.

Cindi and Darlene walked into Jodi's tiny room. There was barely room for all of us. Lauren held Terrence up for both of them to see.

"Terrence!" exclaimed Cindi. "Where did he come from?"

"That's the big mystery!" said Jodi. "Lauren thinks that I took him."

"I do not," said Lauren.

"I don't get it," said Darlene. "Why would Lauren think you took Terrence?"

"Because he showed up in my bookcase," said Jodi.

"I never said that *you* took him," yelled Lauren.

"Yeah, but you *think* I did," accused Jodi.

I couldn't stand to see my teammates fighting. "Stop, everybody!" I shouted. I almost never shout, so I guess when I did it surprised them. Everyone was quiet.

"Listen to me," I said. "Lauren, it couldn't have been Jodi. Remember, we were in this room just a few minutes before the party. Terrence wasn't here."

"He wasn't?" asked Lauren.

Jodi looked at me hopefully. "Hey, you're right," she said.

"You were too upset just now to remember, but I did," I explained.

"Maybe he was here and you didn't notice," said Lauren.

I shook my head. "I'm absolutely sure he wasn't here," I said, realizing I was sticking my neck out, but I *was* sure. I remembered looking at all the trophies in Jodi's bookcase. If fuzzy Terrence had been there, I would have seen him.

"I believe her," said Darlene. "Ti An hasn't got any reason to lie."

"We do have a mystery," I said. "Somebody put Terrence on Jodi's bookshelf."

"Hey, that's right," said Jodi. "Somebody was trying to set me up so that you would all think I had stolen him. See . . . it's proof that it has to be Becky or Ashley. It's the first time either of them has been to my house. They snuck Terrence into my room to make it look like I took him. I'm going right down there now and confront them."

"Me, too," said Lauren. "They're not going to get away with it."

I stood up on the beam. "Hold it . . . just one minute," I said.

"Now what?" Jodi asked impatiently.

"You can't go accusing them again," I said. "Remember what Patrick said in the gym before? He doesn't want any more confrontations."

"But that was before we had *proof*," protested Jodi.

"What proof?" I argued. "We don't have any proof. We have Terrence back, but everybody who was at the meet is here today. All we know is that Terrence wasn't here before the party, and somebody put him here during the party. Anybody could have done it while we were eating the ribs."

"Yeah, but I *know* it was Becky," said Jodi.

"If you go and accuse her now, you'll ruin Barking Barney's party, you'll get Patrick mad at you, and Becky'll just deny it again."

"So what would you have us do, Ti An?" asked

Jodi. "Just let Becky and Ashley get away with it?"

I shook my head. I knew my teammates. I knew they'd never be satisfied with that.

"I have a plan," I said.

"*I've* got a plan. . . . Just bop Becky on the nose," said Jodi.

"Listen to Ti An, Jodi," said Darlene. "She's been right before."

"What if we set a trap?" I suggested. "An elephant trap."

"We don't want to catch an elephant . . . we want to catch a thief," protested Jodi.

I blushed. "Maybe my plan won't work."

"Ti An," said Darlene impatiently, "tell us first and then let us decide."

I told the Pinecones my plan.

"Do you really think it'll work?" demanded Lauren.

"I'm not sure," I admitted.

"At least it's a plan," said Darlene. "It's better than just going on endlessly accusing Becky and Ashley with no proof."

"What should we do about Terrence now?" Lauren asked.

"Let's make the thief squirm," I suggested.

The Pinecones all nodded their heads. "Great idea," said Jodi. "What do you mean?"

"Whoever put Terrence back on your bookshelf

did it because they wanted to see us fighting among ourselves. Let's just pretend that nothing happened. That'll drive them crazy."

We trooped downstairs. Jodi apologized for keeping everybody out of her room. "I had forgotten that my room was such a mess," she said. "I didn't want anybody to see it."

"I can believe that," said Jodi's mom with a laugh.

"Anyhow, the Pinecones helped me clean it up," said Jodi.

"I wasn't there to clean it up," said Ashley. "And I'm a Pinecone."

"You're not a trustworthy Pinecone," said Jodi, glaring at her. I jabbed Jodi in the side with my elbow. Our plan would never work if Jodi picked a fight right away. We needed everything nice and calm until the next meet. Then we'd spring our trap. Only first I had a little science experiment to do. I was glad that the Pinecones had faith in me. Personally I was scared I would fail.

12

Operation Green Dust

In order for my plan to work I needed green chalk dust. Green chalk dust is not something that you can go order from a gymnastics catalog. I got a piece of green solid chalk from the art department at school. I put it between two pieces of paper and started hammering it. My art teacher thought I was very creative. She thought I wanted to see the pattern the chalk dust would leave on the paper.

She was wrong. I was looking for chalk dust that would exactly match Barbie's fur. My whole plan depended on it, and I had told the Pinecones no problem.

Boy, was I wrong. The green was the wrong color, and the chalk dust was all lumpy. Still it was the best I could do. I took the fragments home with me in an envelope.

Dad was correcting papers in the living room. He looked up and smiled at me when I came home. He saw the envelope. "A letter from school?" he asked.

I shook my head quickly. "No, it's an experiment," I answered truthfully.

"Oh, on what?" Dad asked.

"The color green," I said, pleased again that I didn't have to lie.

I took my envelope up to my room and took Barbie from her honored position on my bed.

The two greens didn't match at all. When I dusted her with the chalk dust, Barbie looked like an elephant with light green dandruff. It wasn't Barbie's fault, but I was so frustrated that I threw her across the room.

"I hate this!" I yelled, I guess louder than I thought.

Dad came running up the stairs. "What's wrong?" he asked.

"My experiment failed," I groaned. Dad picked up Barbie and got green dust all over his hands. He looked around for something to wipe his hands on. Finally he had to settle for his T-shirt. He got green handprints all over himself.

"Well, at least that part of the plan will work," I muttered to myself.

Dad looked at me. "Does this experiment have anything to do with crime?" he asked. His eyes

84

were laughing. I don't think of Dad as having much of a sense of humor, even though Mom says that his humor is wicked.

"How did you know?" I asked him.

"It's just a lucky guess," said Dad, laughing. He patted Barbie, and puffs of green chalk dust flew into the air.

"What's the plan?" he asked. "Is it to catch the thief of Lauren's teddy bear?"

"Will you get mad at me?" I asked back. "It's kind of sneaky."

"You have to be sneaky to catch a sneaky thief," said Dad.

"Is that an old Vietnamese saying?" I asked him.

"No," said Dad. "I just made it up."

I told Dad my plan. "The green chalk dust has got to be the right color," I said. "The Pinecones are counting on me, and now I'm going to have to tell them my plan won't work."

"There's always a ton of chalk dust around the gymnasts at your gym," said Dad.

"I know. That's how I thought of it," I said. "But it needs to be green. The chalk dust at the gym is white."

"Food coloring," said Dad. "I can mix the perfect green color. Food coloring will be a new medium for me."

I giggled. "Do you really think you can match

Barbie's color? She's a weird green."

Dad picked her up. "I never noticed it before, but Barbie is the exact shade of a Day-Glo tennis ball. Weird green happens to be one of my specialties," said Dad.

"But even if you can match the color, the food coloring will get the chalk all wet, and then it won't work." My plan, which had seemed so simple when I first thought of it, was getting more and more complicated.

"We'll let the chalk and food coloring dry," said Dad. "Then we'll put it in an airtight bag and save it until you need it." I could tell that Dad was really getting into this plan.

He patted me on the back. "Come on. You get ready for gymnastics, and I'll go down to the kitchen and start playing with the color chart. Be sure to get enough chalk from Patrick so that we can experiment a little." I was beginning to understand what Mom meant when she said that Dad had a wicked sense of humor. Maybe I had inherited a little bit of it.

Dad drove me to gymnastics. He gave me a bag with a drawstring top to take to Patrick's.

"How am I going to get this much?" I asked him.

"I think you're just going to have to ask Patrick," said Dad. "Don't try to steal it."

"I won't," I said, but I couldn't figure out how

I was just going to "ask" Patrick for a big bag of chalk dust.

I was still worrying about this problem when I walked into the gym and into the locker room. Jodi grabbed me. "How's Operation Green Dust?" she whispered out of the corner of her mouth.

"Jodi, hush," I hissed. I looked around. "We've got to act normal until the meet."

"It's hard," said Jodi. "Until we catch the real thief, I'm always going to worry that in the back of Lauren's mind she's wondering if I did it just to be funny."

"Don't worry about it," I said, patting Jodi's arm. Then I realized what I was doing. Me, Ti An, only nine years old, was comforting Jodi and telling her not to worry. It was strange to think of somebody as old and popular as Jodi worrying.

We went out to the gym and did our warm-ups. I kept glancing over at the chalk bin, trying to figure out a way to fill up a plastic bag of chalk dust without Patrick noticing.

I was so busy trying to think up a solution that I did my routines without even thinking about them. I even did the Yamashita vault, and I stuck my landing, but it was as if my mind were a million miles away.

"Ti An, I like the way you're concentrating today," said Patrick after I finished my vault.

I lifted my head. Patrick was hardly ever sarcastic. "I'm sorry," I said quickly. "My head's just not in it today."

Patrick smiled at me. "Well, then, I like where your head was. I mean it. You've been so relaxed in your routines today. Your vault was perfect. I want you to do it just that way in the meet. We'll be in the home gym this weekend. We'll be on our own turf, and with you vaulting like that, we're going to wow the judges."

I stared at him. "I don't remember what I did!" I protested.

"Maybe that's the key to getting Ti An to do well at a competition," said Ashley. "Keep her mind a million miles away."

I knew that Ashley thought she was just being mean, but maybe she did have a point.

"This meet will be a good test," I said. "I'll have plenty to keep my mind occupied."

Patrick laughed as if I were making a joke, except I wasn't being funny.

I bit my lip. I waited until gymnastics was over. Everybody else went to the locker room. Patrick was in the center of the gym checking the equipment the way that he always does both before and after we work out. "Uh, Patrick?" I said quietly to him on the side. "May I ask you a favor?"

"Sure," said Patrick as he tested the tension on the uneven bars. "As long as it doesn't mean trying to get out of Saturday's meet."

"Oh, no," I said quickly. "I wouldn't miss this Saturday's meet for anything."

"Great," said Patrick. "That's the attitude I like to see. Now, tell me, what's the favor."

"May I borrow some chalk dust?" I asked.

Patrick looked at me. " 'Borrow'?" he asked.

"I guess I mean *have* some chalk dust," I admitted. I took out the plastic bag that Dad had given me. "I need it for an art experiment," I added quickly.

"Art experiment?" asked Patrick. "You need quite a bit of it."

I nodded. "My dad's helping me with it."

"Well, in that case . . ." said Patrick, smiling. He filled my plastic bag with chalk dust.

"Thanks," I said, sealing it up.

"Oh, Ti An," said Patrick, "does this 'art experiment' have anything to do with that great old 'art' movie *To Catch a Thief*?"

I stared at Patrick. When did adults get so smart! If our thief was half as smart as Patrick and my dad, my plan was in deep trouble.

13

All We Need
Is the Booby

When I got home, Dad and I set to work. We mixed the chalk dust with Dad's green food coloring. It looked like slime fit for the Ghostbusters. In fact, Dad kept whistling the theme song from *Ghostbusters* the whole time he worked.

"This will never work," I complained.

"Sure it will," said Dad, and he just kept on whistling.

We had to throw away two batches of chalk dust before we got it the right color of green. Then it took forever to dry. Mom came home to see Dad and me hovered over the kitchen table, blowing hot air from her hair dryer into a bag of bright green slime.

"It's an art experiment," said Dad, winking at

me. Mom looked a little bit confused. Dad picked up Barbie, dipped her in a little of the dry green dust, and then handed her to Mom.

"How am I supposed to handle a green dusty elephant?" Mom asked.

"Very gently," said Dad.

Mom laughed. She put Barbie down and then leaned against the kitchen table. "Ugh!" she said, looking down. She had left green hand-prints all over the tablecloth.

"Perfect!" said Dad and I together. Dad gave me a high five. We got chalk dust all over each other.

Mom handed me the Dustbuster. I cleaned up. Dad put the green dust into a Baggie and sealed it. "Keep this safe until it's needed," Dad said to me.

"I don't suppose anybody wants to tell me what's going on?" Mom asked.

Dad and I both grinned and shook our heads. I couldn't remember ever having such a good time with my dad. I had always loved him, but I never thought of him as somebody who could be fun.

On Saturday, I carefully packed the green bag into the inside pocket of my knapsack. Then I put Barbie into my knapsack headfirst. Mom and Dad were both coming to the meet.

"Good luck, honey," Mom said to me at the

gym as I headed for the locker room with my knapsack.

"She has Barbie today," said Dad. "That's all the luck she needs."

Mom looked at Dad strangely.

"Dad, you're wicked," I said to him.

Dad nodded to me solemnly, and then he gave me a wink. Dad *really* was wicked fun.

In the locker room, I brought out Barbie and introduced her to everyone. "This is Barbie, my elephant. She's going to bring us all good luck," I said.

Lauren winked at me. It was getting to be Wink City around the gym that day. I hoped all the winks wouldn't give us away.

"A green elephant!" exclaimed Becky. "He's a disgusting color. He's even more embarrassing than Lauren's teddy bear."

"He is a she," I corrected Becky. "She's named 'Barbie,' after the doll."

"Your good-luck charm is named after the Barbie doll?" snorted Becky. "You can't take her out onto the floor."

"Oh, yeah?" I said, hitting the swinging door to our locker room with my shoulder. "Just watch me."

The Pinecones followed me as we took Barbie out to show the boys' team. In a voice loud enough for all the Atomic Amazons to hear me,

I took Barbie around to Jared, Ryan, and the others and told them to pat Barbie for good luck.

Jodi's mom looked at Barbie a little curiously. "Wasn't the Pinecones good-luck charm a teddy bear?" she asked.

"Oh, Barbie's even more good luck," I assured her.

"It's a proven fact," said Lauren as we went around the gym making sure that everybody saw Barbie, and everybody heard us say that she brought us good luck.

Patrick blew his whistle. It was the signal for all the Pinecones to gather around him for our final warm-up.

Patrick started to give us our pre-meet pep talk. I raised my arm. "I'm so nervous. I've got to go to the bathroom," I whispered.

"Go on, Ti An," said Patrick. "Nerves are good for you."

Lauren winked at me again, as I picked up Barbie and took her with me into the bathroom. I wished that Lauren would stop winking.

I took my knapsack into the stall with me, and took out the green package. I dusted Barbie all over with the green chalk, being careful that any loose dust fell into the toilet. If anybody had looked into the toilet stall and had seen what I was doing, they would have thought I was nuts.

I carefully carried Barbie by the inside of her

ears back to the gym. If I'd sneezed, I would have been green all over. I put her down on an old vaulting horse pushed against the wall. She looked exactly the same as she had without the chalk dust. And she was hard to miss — a green elephant perched on a horse.

I sat back down cross-legged and tried to concentrate on Patrick's pep talk, but my heart wasn't in it. All I could think of was Barbie sitting on the vault, an innocent-looking booby trap. Now all we needed was the booby.

14

Green With Envy

We completed our warm-ups. I didn't have a chance to watch Barbie every moment, but after we finished I looked over at the horse. There was nothing there but a little ring of green dust.

The judges were just setting up. Usually the longest time during a meet seems to be the time between when we finish our warm-ups and when the meet actually starts. Now I was worried there wouldn't be enough time.

I ran and got Lauren and told her that "the trap was sprung."

"Now what?" she asked excitedly.

"Now we find green dust all over Ashley's or Becky's leotard," said Jodi, coming up to me. She had noticed that Barbie was missing, too.

"We'll catch them green-handed," said Cindi, excitedly.

"Ti An and I will go look at Ashley," said Lauren, taking over my plan. "Darlene, Jodi, and Cindi go see Becky."

"Be careful . . ." I started to warn them, but I knew now was not the time to tell them to be subtle.

Lauren and I went over to where Ashley was nervously pacing in front of the beam. She paced up and down, giving us a chance to get a good look at her.

"She doesn't have green chalk dust on her!" exclaimed Lauren.

"She looks clean to me," I admitted.

"It must be Becky, then," said Lauren. "Come on." She grabbed my arm.

Becky always likes to concentrate by herself before a meet. Her white Evergreen uniform was as clean as fresh fallen snow.

"What are you looking for?" Becky asked, annoyed as all the Pinecones gathered around her.

"You didn't just change leotards, did you?" Lauren asked.

"Go back to your stuffed animals," said Becky. "I've got a meet to get ready for."

Cindi and Jodi looked at me. "We'd better leave her alone," I whispered. We tiptoed away.

"Your trap failed," hissed Jodi to me.

"We should never have left it all up to Ti An," said Lauren. "She's just a kid."

"You're right," said Jodi. "It's not your fault, Ti An."

"Wait a minute, you guys," I protested. "I said the trap would give us proof; I never said it would be the proof you wanted."

"What does that mean?" demanded Lauren.

"Look!" I said. I pointed across the gym to where Nick was standing in the corner, slapping his shorts with his hands. He looked like he was trying to slap away a swarm of mosquitoes.

"What is that creep doing now?" Jodi asked.

"He's trying to get the green dust off his hands, that's what he's doing!" I exclaimed.

I looked back at the judges' table. Coach Miller and Patrick were both occupied talking to the judges.

"Come on!" I yelled. "Before Nick gets it all off."

We shot over to the boys' corner. Nick had green dust all over him.

"What's the matter, Nick?" asked Jodi. "Did you get slimed?"

Nick looked to his left and then to his right. We had him surrounded.

"You little pest, you deserve to turn green."

"How did you know it was me?" Nick whined.

"Ti An figured it out," said Lauren.

Nick giggled nervously. "I just took Terrence

as a joke. You all were going on and on about how much luck he brought you, and then the boys' Evergreen team beat our team. He didn't bring you any luck, but I figured that maybe he would help us. He didn't, so I put him back where I knew you'd find him."

"You put him back where you thought *I'd* get in trouble," said Jodi.

"Yeah, I did, didn't I?" admitted Nick. He sounded sorry that he was caught but not the least bit sorry that he did it.

"You took Barbie, just because you thought *she'd* bring you luck. Well, she did . . . bad luck," said Lauren.

Suddenly Patrick stepped into the middle of our circle. "Would somebody please tell me what's going on?" he demanded. "We are supposed to be having a meet here today."

"It was *Nick*," said Jodi. "He took Terrence and then he tried to take Barbie. I told everybody he was a pest."

"Ti An was the one who kept telling us we needed proof," said Lauren. "We all thought it had to be Ashley or Becky. It wasn't either of them. Thanks to Ti An, we set a trap, and Nick walked right into it."

"I'm grateful to Ti An," said Patrick. "But, Pinecones, we have more important things to worry about than lost teddy bears and silly pranks. Remember, we have a meet starting in about three minutes. I would like you to regroup and think about that."

"But what about Nick?" Jodi demanded.

"Nick, where is Ti An's elephant?" Patrick demanded.

"He's right on the Amazons' bench," said Nick. "I took him over there and told all the Amazons to pat him for good luck."

Patrick looked over at the Amazons' bench. They were all looking down at their hands. All their bright red uniforms were spotted with green.

A big smile came over Patrick's face. "Nick," he said, "I think you'd better go over to Coach Miller and explain to him why all his gymnasts are turning green."

Nick started to turn green himself.

"I think confessing to Coach Miller that you're to blame for the Amazons turning green with envy will be punishment enough," said Patrick.

I had to agree. I wouldn't have been in Nick's shoes for anything.

"All right, Pinecones," said Patrick. "Maybe *now* you're ready to win a meet."

I wished Patrick hadn't said that. I was so enjoying watching the Atomic Amazons suffer. Now we had to get back to reality.

15

Nowhere to Go but Up

The announcer got on the loudspeaker. "The meet will begin in exactly two minutes," he said. "We will start with the vault. Our first vaulter will be Ti An Truong."

Patrick looked down at me. He was herding all the Pinecones back across the floor toward the vault. He put his arm around me. "Thanks for solving the mystery for the Pinecones," he said. "Now maybe everybody will be able to keep their minds on the meet instead of on revenge."

"I kept telling them that we needed proof," I said proudly.

Patrick nodded. "It couldn't have been easy standing up to Jodi and Lauren once they had their minds made up. I know those two. It takes a lot to convince them they're wrong."

"I didn't believe the first thing I heard," I explained to Patrick.

"And what about in competition?" he said. "That's another place where I want you to challenge your beliefs."

I looked up at Patrick. "I don't understand."

"Ti An, think about why you do so well in practice but have trouble in competition."

"That's just me," I argued. "That's the way I am."

"No, it isn't," Patrick said. "Until today, I don't think you realized how important you are to the team. I think you have trouble believing how much you count. You don't have to be perfect. You just have to believe that what you do matters."

I looked over at the audience. My father was watching me talking to Patrick. I thought about the way my dad did *everything* as if it were important. Even when he was helping me make green chalk dust, he worked as hard on getting it exactly right as if it were a history paper he was writing or a marathon he was running. Maybe I was a little bit more like my father than I realized. I thought about Dad's wicked sense of humor and his pride. I decided that being like my dad might not be all bad.

"If you were big enough to stand up to Jodi

and Lauren when they thought they knew who took Lauren's teddy bear," said Patrick, "you're big enough to stand up to the Amazons."

The judges called my name. "Come on, Ti An," said Patrick. "Do the Yamashita vault. Remember how well you did it in practice before? Let's give the Atomic Amazons something to really be green about."

"Do you honestly think I can do it?" I asked him.

"I *know* you can do it in practice," said Patrick. "I *believe* you're ready to do it now that it counts."

I took a deep breath. I heard the Pinecones shouting my name. "Go, Ti An! Ti An! TI AN! If she can't do it, nobody can!"

I shook my arms out to try to release some of the tension.

I saluted the judges. I ran for the horse as fast as I could. I hit the springboard just a little bit off center. I sprang for the handspring and tried to push up into the pike position for the Yamashita, but I didn't have enough height. I landed with a thud on my backside. I rolled over on my hip. I hit it hard, and I knew it was going to be black and blue in the morning. The entire audience was silent. I stood up and saluted the judges to show that I could finish the vault, but I knew that my score was going to be low.

I walked back over to the Pinecones. "Are you okay, Ti An?" Lauren asked worriedly.

"I'm okay," I said.

"Are you sure?" Patrick asked me.

"Sorry I fouled up," I said.

"You've got a second vault," said Patrick.

"Yeah, but she's going to do the easier vault, isn't she?" asked Ashley. "You're not going to let Ti An try the Yamashita again in competition."

"It's up to Ti An," said Patrick.

"You don't have to do it, Ti An," said Darlene.

Lauren didn't say anything. She hadn't mastered the Yamashita, and I knew she'd never try it in competition.

The judges announced the score for my first vault. It was a 4.8. It was way too low if I was going to really help my team.

I walked to the edge of the runway to get ready for my second vault.

Lauren came hurrying up to me. She had Terrence under one arm and Barbie under the other. She had green chalk dust all over her white Evergreen uniform.

"Touch them both for good luck!" Lauren insisted.

"You're turning green," I told her.

"The dust will come off," said Lauren. "The good luck will stay."

I tapped both Terrence and Barbie on the head.

I carefully wiped the green dust off on my gymnast towel.

The judge signaled me to start. I returned her signal to show I was ready. I realized I was as ready as I would ever be.

I ran down the approach thinking about nothing except hitting the springboard on center. The springboard made a great cracking sound as I hit it just right.

My hands barely touched the horse. I bounced up and into the air, my legs straight and together, my body tight, and my toes pointed.

I rebounded almost six feet away from the horse. A good vault meant that I would have traveled at least the length of my body, which in my case is just under four feet. I had gone two feet beyond my own height. My knees bent and I had to take a step forward, but I didn't fall. Both my arms were high over my head, not because I was trying to give a victory salute, but because I was still struggling to keep my balance after the force of the Yamashita.

I could hear the Pinecones cheering like crazy behind me. I knew even before I got the judges' score that I had done the vault of my life.

After I saluted the judge officially, Patrick ran out onto the mat and gave me a big hug.

We turned and waited for the judges' score. Patrick was blocking my view, and I didn't see

the score at first. I heard the Atomic Amazons'
bench gasp, and I knew they were in trouble.

Patrick moved out of the way so that I could
have a clear view of the score. 9.4. It was un-
believable!

"The Pinecones have nowhere to go but up,"
said Patrick happily, as he took me back over to
the bench with the other Pinecones. "Sometimes
number one really is number one."

"And she's a good detective, too," said Lauren.

"Who says you can only be number one in one
thing?" asked Patrick.

I looked over at my father and waved happily
to him for the video camera. My dad isn't good
at only one thing, and neither am I. I guess we
are more alike than I realized. This was one videotape that I knew I would want to keep. Forever.

About the Author

Elizabeth Levy decided that the only way she could write about gymnastics was to try it herself. Besides taking classes she is involved with a group of young gymnasts near her home in New York City, and enjoys following their progress.

Elizabeth Levy's other Apple Paperbacks are *A Different Twist, The Computer That Said Steal Me*, and all the other books in THE GYMNASTS series.

She likes visiting schools to give talks and meet her readers. Kids love her presentation's opening. Why? "I start with a cartwheel!" says Levy. "At least I try to."